Pencil
DOG

FoR Granny AND Grandpa & DEAR Eebee (who had the good idea).

SIMON & SCHUSTER
First published in Great Britain in 2019 by Simon & Schuster UK Ltd
1st Floor, 222 Gray's Inn Road, London WC1X 8HB
A CBS Company
Text and illustrations copyright © 2019 Leigh Hodgkinson
The right of Leigh Hodgkinson to be identified as the author and illustrator of
this work has been asserted by her in accordance with the Copyright, Designs and Patents Act, 1988
A CIP catalogue record for this book is available from the British Library upon request
ISBN: 978-1-4711-6939-7 (HB) • ISBN: 978-1-4711-6940-3 (PB) • ISBN: 978-1-4711-6941-0 (eBook)
Printed in China • 10 9 8 7 6 5 4 3 2 1

Pencil DOG

Leigh Hodgkinson

SIMON & SCHUSTER
London New York Sydney Toronto New Delhi

This is me and Pencil Dog.
We love to spend time with each other.

It's not just the time that flies when we are together –
we do too!
With Pencil Dog, ANYTHING is possible.

wherever we go!

Pencil Dog always has the most WONDERFUL stories right at the tip of his nose.

But the BEST thing about Pencil Dog
is that he is ALWAYS there to catch me when I . . .

. . . fall.

Oh dear –
well, he usually is.

Pencil Dog?

Pencil Dog,
where are you?

We were in
the middle of
a story . . .

you NEVER leave in
the middle of a story.

And then
I find him –

fast asleep and snoring.
Dear little Pencil Dog is all worn out.

Even though he's not as sharp as he used to be,
I don't mind ONE bit.

Luckily, I'm around to find adventures
and help tell stories . . .

like the time Pencil Dog flew over the mountains in a colourful hot-air balloon! Or when he lived in a tiny tent under the twinkling stars and ate toasted

marshmallows for breakfast. Or the time he fell in love under the biggest rainbow . . .

Then, one day, Pencil Dog gets so very small,
he actually disappears.

He isn't here any more.
I miss him terribly.

But slowly, I realise that I still have so much of him with me.

So Pencil Dog hasn't disappeared completely.

And in a way,
he never will.